Anne of Green Gables

My First Classics

A Little Princess

by Frances Hodgson Burnett,
adapted by Laura F. Marsh

The Secret Garden

by Frances Hodgson Burnett,
adapted by Laura F. Marsh

Anne of Green Gables

By L. M. Montgomery

Adapted by Laura F. Marsh

≡ HarperFestival®

A Division of HarperCollinsPublishers

HarperCollins®, ☎®, and HarperFestival® are trademarks of
HarperCollins Publishers, Inc.

My First Classics: Anne of Green Gables
© 2005 by HarperCollins Publishers
Printed in the United States of America. For information address
HarperCollins Children's Books, a division of HarperCollins
Publishers, 1350 Avenue of the Americas, New York, NY 10019.
www.harperchildrens.com
Library of Congress catalog card number: 2004115866
Typography by Al Cetta
1 2 3 4 5 6 7 8 9 10
❖
First HarperFestival edition, 2005

Contents

Anne of Green Gables

~ 1 ~

Mrs. Rachel Lynde Is Surprised

Mrs. Rachel Lynde was sitting at her window watching the main road by her house. Anyone who went in or out of Avonlea had to pass before her eyes. On this June day, Mrs. Lynde saw Matthew Cuthbert drive by with his horse and buggy. He wore his best suit. *Where is Matthew going and why?* Mrs. Lynde thought to herself.

Matthew was perhaps the shyest man alive. He rarely left home because he didn't like to be among strangers. Since Mrs. Lynde could not have any peace until she knew Matthew's business, she decided to go to the Cuthberts' house to find out.

Mrs. Lynde walked to the big rambling house that sat among the orchards. The house, called Green Gables, was set back on the farthest edge of the cleared land and was owned by Matthew and his sister, Marilla. *It's no wonder Matthew and Marilla are both a little odd, living way back here by themselves*, thought Mrs. Lynde. She had opinions about everything.

When Mrs. Lynde entered the kitchen, she found

Marilla Cuthbert knitting. "Good evening, Rachel," Marilla said to her neighbor. "Won't you sit down? How is your family?" The two women were friends despite how very different they were.

Mrs. Lynde noticed that the table was set for tea, but instead of two place settings, there were three. *Matthew must be bringing home a guest*, she thought.

"We are all well," replied Mrs. Lynde. "Though I was afraid you were not when I saw Matthew leaving today. I thought maybe he was going for the doctor."

Marilla had been expecting Mrs. Lynde. She knew seeing Matthew leave would be too much for her curiosity. "Oh, I'm well," Marilla replied. "Matthew went to Bright River. We're getting a little boy from an orphan asylum. He's coming on the train tonight."

Mrs. Lynde was very surprised. "What put this idea in your heads?" she said when she could speak again. Mrs. Lynde had not been asked her opinion on this decision, and so she did not approve.

"Well, we've been thinking about it for a long time," Marilla replied. "Mrs. Spencer is adopting a girl from the asylum. And Matthew is getting older—he's sixty—and his heart troubles him. We thought a little boy of about ten or eleven could do chores, but would be young enough to be trained up proper. We asked Mrs. Spencer to pick us out a little boy when she went for her girl."

Mrs. Lynde always spoke her mind. "Well, Marilla, I think what you're doing is mighty foolish. You don't know a thing about this child. Why, last week I read in the paper about a boy from an orphan asylum that set fire to the house—on purpose. If you had asked my advice—which you didn't—I'd have said not to do it."

"I've had questions myself," Marilla said, "but Matthew was set on it. And as for the risk, there's risk in everything we do."

"Well, I hope it turns out all right," said Mrs. Lynde. As she walked down the lane, Mrs. Lynde said to herself, *Matthew and Marilla don't know anything about children. I'm sorry for the poor young one, that's for sure.*

~ 2 ~
Matthew Cuthbert
Is Surprised

When Matthew Cuthbert arrived at the train station, the platform was empty. He found the stationmaster locking up. "The five-thirty train came and went," said the official. "But there was a passenger dropped off for you. She's sitting over there."

"But I'm not expecting a girl," said Matthew blankly.

"Must be some mistake," the stationmaster said. "Mrs. Spencer brought her off the train. That's all I know." Then he walked away.

Matthew shuffled slowly toward the girl. She had been watching Matthew. She was about eleven years old and wore a very tight, short dress of yellowish gray and a faded brown hat. She had two braids of thick red hair down her back. Her face was small and thin with freckles, and her eyes were very large.

When the child saw Matthew approach, she stood up and put out her hand to him. "I suppose you are Matthew Cuthbert of Green Gables?" she said in a clear, sweet voice. "I'm very glad to see you. I was beginning to think you weren't coming."

Matthew quickly decided what to do. He could not tell this child with the eager eyes that there had been a mistake. He would take her home and let Marilla do that. The girl couldn't be left at the train station anyway. "I'm sorry I'm late," he said shyly. "Come along. The horse is over here."

"Oh, it is so wonderful that I am going to live with you and belong to you!" she said. "I've never belonged to anybody. I only lived at the asylum for four months, but that was enough."

The little girl stopped talking once they reached the buggy, and she remained quiet during the first part of the drive. They passed by trees of cherry, white birch, and wild plum. "Isn't that beautiful?" she asked. "What did that white and lacy tree make you think of?"

"Well now, I dunno," said Matthew.

"Why, a bride—dressed in white with a lovely misty veil! I don't ever expect to be a bride. I'm so homely nobody will want to marry me. I do hope to have a pretty white dress someday. I've never had a pretty dress in my life. I've always imagined I lived on Prince Edward Island, but I never really expected to. It's delightful when your imaginations come true. Am I talking too much?"

Much to his surprise, Matthew was enjoying himself. He said shyly, "You can talk as much as you like. I don't mind."

"I'm so glad. I know you and I are going to get along fine," she said. "People laugh at me because I use big words. But if you have big ideas, you need big words to express them, don't you?"

"Well now, that seems reasonable," said Matthew.

"Mrs. Spencer said your place is named Green Gables. She said there were trees all around it. Is there a brook near the house?"

"Well, yes, there is one below the house," Matthew replied.

"Fancy! It's always been one of my dreams to live near a brook. Now I feel nearly perfectly happy. I can't feel *perfectly* happy because—well, what color would you say this is?" She grabbed one of her braids and held it up to Matthew.

"It's red, ain't it?" he replied.

The girl dropped the braid with a deep sigh that seemed to come from her toes. "Yes, it's red," she said sadly. "Now you see why I can't be perfectly happy. I can imagine some things away. But I *cannot* imagine red hair away. I read once—Oh, Mr. Cuthbert!"

They had rounded a curve and come upon the "Avenue," a place where large blossoming apple trees arched over the road to meet each other. The beauty of

8

the Avenue made the child speechless. She had not moved or spoken even after they were three miles down the road.

"Mr. Cuthbert," she said at last. "What *was* that white place we came through?"

"Well, you must mean the Avenue," he answered.

"It's wonderful! But they should call it—the White Way of Delight. When I don't like a name, I always imagine a new one."

They drove over the crest of a hill and below them were a pond and a bridge. Beyond that was the dark blue of the gulf.

"That's Barry's pond," said Matthew.

"Oh, I don't like that name either," she said. "I shall call it—the Lake of Shining Waters. Yes, that is the right name for it."

"We're almost home now," Matthew said. "That's Green Gables over—"

"Oh, don't tell me," she interrupted, shutting her eyes. "Let me guess." She looked around and settled her eyes on a house set back from the road. "That's it, isn't it?"

"Well now, you've guessed it!" cried Matthew.

"As soon as I saw it, I felt it was home." With a sigh, she sat back in silence. Matthew felt very uneasy. But he was glad that he wouldn't have to tell her that the home she wanted so badly was not going to be hers after all.

By the time they arrived at the house, Matthew was very worried. It was not of Marilla or himself he was thinking now, but of the child's disappointment. The girl followed him into the house, tightly holding her bag as she went.

~ 3 ~
Marilla Cuthbert
Is Surprised

Marilla met them at the door. As her eyes fell on the odd little girl with big eyes, she stopped short.

"Matthew, who's that?" she asked. "Where is the boy?"

"There wasn't any boy," he responded.

"But there must have been a boy," insisted Marilla. "We sent word for Mrs. Spencer to bring a boy."

"Well, she brought *her*," Matthew said. "I questioned the stationmaster. I had to bring her home. She couldn't be left there."

"Well, this is a pretty mess!" cried Marilla.

While Matthew and Marilla were talking, the child had been silent. Now her face showed that she understood what had happened. "You don't want me because I'm not a boy!" she cried. "I should have expected it. Nobody has ever wanted me. I should have known it was all too beautiful to last. Oh, what shall I do?"

She burst into tears and buried her face in her arms. Marilla and Matthew looked at each other. They did not know what to do. Finally Marilla said, "Well, there's no need to cry."

"Oh, yes there is!" the child said with trembling lips. "You would cry too if you were an orphan and came to a place you thought would be home and then found out they didn't want you. Oh, this is the most *tragical* thing that has ever happened to me!"

A small smile, rusty from too little use, crossed Marilla's lips. "Well, don't cry," she said. "We won't turn you away tonight. You'll stay here until we straighten this out. What's your name?"

"Will you please call me Cordelia?" asked the child eagerly.

"*Call* you Cordelia? Is that your name?" asked Marilla.

"No—not exactly," she replied. "But I would love to be called Cordelia. It's such an elegant name."

"If Cordelia isn't your name, what is it?"

"Anne Shirley," the little girl said slowly. "But if you must call me Anne, please call me Anne spelled with an *e*. It looks so much more distinguished."

"Very well, Anne spelled with an *e*," Marilla answered. "Can you tell me how this mistake was made?"

"Mrs. Spencer distinctly said you wanted a girl about eleven years old and she thought I would do. I couldn't sleep I was so excited. If I was beautiful and had brown hair, would you keep me?"

"No," said Marilla flatly. "We want a boy to help Matthew on the farm. Now take off your hat and we'll sit down to supper."

Matthew came in meekly and sat down at the table. Anne could not eat. She nibbled at the bread in front of her.

"You're not eating anything," Marilla noted.

"I can't," said Anne. "I'm in the depths of despair. Can you eat when you are in the depths of despair?"

"I've never been in the depths of despair, so I can't say," replied Marilla.

"Well, a lump is in your throat and you can't swallow anything, not even if it was a chocolate caramel," Anne explained. "I had one two years ago and it was simply delicious. I hope you won't be offended that I can't eat anything."

"She's probably tired," said Matthew. "Best put her to bed."

Marilla lit a candle and led Anne upstairs to a room in the east gable. It was very neat and clean like the rest of the house.

"Well, undress quick and get to bed," Marilla said. "I'll come back in a few minutes for the candle."

Anne looked around the room when Marilla was gone. The floor and the walls were bare. There was a high, old-fashioned bed in the corner. As she took off her garments, Anne let a sob escape her. She sprang into bed and buried her face in the pillow.

When Marilla came back in, she went over to the bed. "Good night," Marilla said awkwardly, but not unkindly. Marilla went downstairs to do the dishes. Matthew looked as if he had something on his mind.

"That's what we get for not going to the asylum ourselves," Marilla said. "The girl will have to be sent back."

"I suppose so," Matthew said.

"You *suppose* so?" Marilla stood looking at him in disbelief.

"Well now, she's a real nice little thing, Marilla. It's kind of a pity to send her back when she's so set on staying here."

"What good would she be to us?" Marilla said.

"We might be some good to her," said Matthew suddenly. "She's an interesting thing. You should have heard her talk coming from the station."

"Oh, I can see she can talk fast," said Marilla. "I don't like children who have so much to say."

"I could hire a French boy to help me," Matthew offered.

"I'm not going to keep her," Marilla said shortly.

"Well now, I'm going to bed." So Matthew went upstairs.

In the east gable, a child cried herself to sleep.

~ 4 ~
Morning at Green Gables

It was late morning when Anne awoke. When she went to look out her window, her eyes glistened with delight. On both sides of the house was a big orchard of cherry and apple trees. It was beautiful outside. Since Anne had seen so many ugly places in her life, she could barely take her eyes away from the window.

Anne was startled by Marilla's hand on her shoulder. "It's time to get dressed," she said. Marilla did not know how to talk to a child and so she sounded unfriendly. But she did not mean to be.

Anne stood up. "Oh, isn't it wonderful?" she said, waving her hand at the outside world. "I shall always remember that brook even if I never see it again. I've just been imagining it was really me you wanted all along and that I could stay here forever. It was a great comfort while it lasted."

"Dress and come downstairs for breakfast," Marilla said.

In about ten minutes, Anne was downstairs. "I'm so glad it's a sunshiny morning," she said. "It's easier to bear sadness on a sunshiny day. It's all very well to

15

read about sorrows and imagine yourself living through them, but it's not nice when you really do have them, is it?"

"For pity's sake, hold your tongue," said Marilla. "You talk entirely too much for a little girl."

So Anne was quiet, and her silence made Marilla nervous. It seemed almost unnatural. Matthew was also quiet, as usual, so the meal was a silent one.

Marilla could see that Matthew wanted to keep Anne just as much this morning as he had last night. He had not said a word on the subject, but Marilla knew this without being told.

After breakfast Marilla said to Anne, "We'll see Mrs. Spencer and settle what's to be done with you. Now you may play outside."

When Anne finished the dishes, she flew to the door with a thrilled expression on her face. But then she stopped and came back.

"What's the matter now?" asked Marilla.

"I don't dare go out," replied Anne in a sad tone. "If I can't stay here, there is no use in my loving Green Gables."

"I have never in all my life heard anything equal to her," muttered Marilla. But she thought to herself, *She is kind of interesting, as Matthew says. I'm wondering what she will say next.*

When Marilla asked Matthew for the buggy in the

afternoon, Matthew looked over at Anne sadly. "I'm going to talk with Mrs. Spencer and settle this thing," Marilla said to him. "She will probably make arrangements to send her back to Nova Scotia at once. I'll be home to milk the cows."

Matthew said nothing.

The buggy was hitched, and Marilla and Anne set off in the afternoon. Matthew opened the gate and said, "Little Jerry Buote was here this morning, and I told him I'd hire him for the summer."

Marilla made no reply and started the horses in a hurry. As she glanced back at Matthew, she saw that he looked longingly after them down the road.

~ 5 ~
Anne's History

"I've made up my mind to enjoy this drive," Anne said to Marilla. "I'm not going to think about going back to the asylum just now. Oh, what a lovely pink rose. I can't wear it because of my red hair. Do you know anyone whose hair was red when she was young, but changed color when she grew up?"

"No, I don't know that I did," said Marilla.

Anne sighed. "Well, that's another hope gone. My life is a graveyard of buried hopes. That's a sentence I read in a book. It's so romantic that it makes me feel comforted."

They drove farther down the road. "Why don't you tell me what you know about yourself?" asked Marilla.

"What I *know* about myself isn't really worth telling," said Anne. "But what I *imagine* about myself is."

"No, I don't want any imaginings. Just stick to the facts. Where were you born and how old are you?"

"I was eleven last March," said Anne with a sigh. "And I was born in Bolingbroke, Nova Scotia. My parents were Walter and Bertha Shirley, and they were teachers at the high school. They lived in a little house in town. Mrs. Thomas said I was the homeliest baby she ever saw, but that Mother thought I was beautiful. I'm glad she was satisfied with me, because she didn't live long after that. She died of fever when I was three months old. And Father died four days after, from fever, too. That left me an orphan and folks were at their wits' end what to do with me. You see, nobody wanted me even then. Father and Mother had come from other places and didn't have any living relatives. Finally Mrs. Thomas said she'd take me, though she was poor.

"I lived with Mr. and Mrs. Thomas until I was eight years old. I helped look after the Thomas children— there were four younger than me. Then Mr. Thomas was killed by a train and his mother took Mrs. Thomas and the children, but she didn't want me. Then Mrs. Hammond from up the river took me, seeing I was handy with children. Mrs. Hammond had eight children—twins three times. I used to get dreadfully tired carrying them about.

"I lived with Mrs. Hammond for two years, and then Mr. Hammond died and Mrs. Hammond divided her children among her relatives and went to the States. I had to go to the orphan asylum then. They didn't want me there either because they were full. But they had to take me. I was there four months until Mrs. Spencer came."

Anne finished with another sigh. She did not like

talking about her life in a world that had not wanted her.

"Did you ever go to school?" Marilla asked.

"Not much. I can read pretty well and I know many pieces of poetry by heart."

"Were those women—Mrs. Thomas and Mrs. Hammond—good to you?" asked Marilla, looking at Anne carefully.

"O-o-o-h," stammered Anne. "They meant to be— I know they meant to be just as good and kind as possible."

Marilla asked no more questions. Pity for Anne was stirring in her heart as she drove over the shore road. What a starved, unloved life Anne had had—a life of poverty and neglect. No wonder she had been so happy at the thought of a real home. It was a pity she had to be sent back. *But what if I were to let Anne stay? She seems like a nice, teachable little thing. She's got too much to say,* Marilla thought. *But she might be trained out of that. And there's nothing rude about what she does.*

"What is that big house ahead?" Anne said after a while.

"That's the White Sands Hotel," said Marilla.

"I was afraid it was Mrs. Spencer's place," replied Anne. "Getting there will somehow seem like the end of everything."

~ 6 ~
Marilla Makes Up Her Mind

When they arrived at Mrs. Spencer's house, Mrs. Spencer was surprised to see them.

"Mrs. Spencer, I'm afraid there's been a mistake," Marilla said. "We told your brother for you to bring us a boy from the asylum."

"You don't say so!" cried Mrs. Spencer. "Robert's daughter Nancy said that you wanted a girl. I'm sorry."

"Well, we should have gone ourselves," said Marilla. "Now the only thing to do is to set it right. Can we send the child back?"

"Well, perhaps. But Mrs. Peter Blewett was here yesterday, and she needs help with all her children. Anne could be the very girl."

Marilla had heard tales of Mrs. Blewett's temper and stinginess, and about her quarrelsome children. She felt uneasy about handing over Anne to this woman.

"Well, if it isn't Mrs. Blewett walking up the lane this minute!" said Mrs. Spencer. "We can settle the matter right away."

When Mrs. Blewett entered, Anne saw that she was a sharp-faced, sharp-eyed woman. She felt a lump rising in her throat. Mrs. Spencer explained the situation. "So, if you're still in need of help," said Mrs. Spencer, "I think Anne will be just the thing for you."

"How old are you and what is your name?" Mrs. Blewett demanded. Anne answered shakily, shrinking down into her chair.

"Humpf!" Mrs. Blewett replied. "You don't look like much. But you're wiry, and the wiry ones are the best. I'll expect you to earn your keep. Yes, I will take her off your hands, Miss Cuthbert. I can take her right now."

Marilla looked at Anne and softened at the sight of the child's misery. She felt if she ignored Anne's sad face, it would haunt her for the rest of her life. Moreover, Marilla did not like Mrs. Blewett.

"Well, I don't know," Marilla replied. "I didn't say we had decided yet. In fact, Matthew would like to keep her. I'd better take her home and talk it over with him."

Mrs. Blewett was not pleased, but she agreed. When the two ladies left the room, Anne almost flew over to Marilla. "Oh, Miss Cuthbert, did you really say that you might let me stay at Green Gables?"

"Yes, I did say that, but it isn't decided yet and perhaps Mrs. Blewett will take you after all."

"I'd rather go back to the asylum than go live with her," Anne said passionately. "She looks like a gimlet."

Marilla smothered a smile. "You should not talk that way about a lady and a stranger," she told Anne.

"I'll try to be everything you want me to be if you'll keep me," Anne replied.

When they arrived back at Green Gables, Matthew met them in the lane. Marilla could see the relief in his face. That night she told him Anne's history and the result of the visit with Mrs. Spencer.

"I would not give a dog I liked to Mrs. Blewett," said Matthew.

"Well, since you seem to want her," Marilla said, "I suppose I'm willing. I'm getting kind of used to the idea. I've never brought up a child, and I dare say I'll make a terrible mess of it. But I'll do my best. She may stay."

Matthew's shy face was a glow of delight. "She's such an interesting thing," he said again.

"It would be better if she were a useful thing," Marilla responded. "But I'll see to it she's trained to be that. Now, Matthew, you are not to interfere with my methods. You just leave me to manage her."

"There, there, Marilla," he responded. "You'll have your way. Only be as good and kind to her as you can."

"I won't tell her tonight that she can stay," Marilla

said, "for she'd be too excited to sleep. Did you ever think we'd adopt an orphan girl? It certainly is surprising that you're at the bottom of this, Matthew Cuthbert, since you've always avoided girls."

~ 7 ~
Bringing Up Anne

The next morning Marilla had decided that Anne was smart, willing to work, and quick to learn. However, Anne quickly fell into daydreams in the middle of what she was doing.

After lunch Anne came to Marilla trembling from head to foot. "Oh, please, Miss Cuthbert, won't you tell me if you are going to send me away or not? I cannot bear not knowing a moment longer."

"Well," said Marilla, "Matthew and I have decided to keep you—if you will try to be a good girl. Why, child, what is the matter?"

Anne was crying. "I'm so happy," she said. "I'll try to be good. It will be uphill work, I expect, for Mrs. Thomas often told me I was desperately wicked. But I'll do my best."

"You can stay," Marilla said, "and we'll try to do right by you. You will go to school in September, and you can call me Marilla."

"Marilla," Anne asked, "do you think I'll ever have a bosom friend in Avonlea?"

"A what kind of friend?" Marilla said.

"A bosom friend—someone I can talk to about

everything. A kindred spirit," Anne explained. "I've dreamed of having such a friend all my life. Do you think it's possible?"

"Diana Barry lives over at Orchard Slope, and she's about your age. Perhaps she will be a playmate for you. You'll have to be careful, though. Mrs. Barry won't let Diana play with anyone who isn't nice and good."

"What is Diana like?" asked Anne. "I just love her name."

"She is very pretty," said Marilla. "And she is smart, too."

"Oh, it would be wonderful to have a bosom friend," Anne said. "I used to have a make-believe friend named Katie Maurice when I was at Mrs. Thomas's house. I talked to her for hours."

"It will be good for you to have a real friend to put such nonsense out of your head," replied Marilla.

Mrs. Rachel Lynde Is Horrified

Anne had been at Green Gables only one night before Mrs. Rachel Lynde came to inspect her. In this time Anne had already explored the orchard, the bridge, the brook, and every tree and shrub around the house. Matthew listened to Anne's explorations with a smile on his face.

"I've been hearing some surprising things about you and Matthew," Mrs. Lynde said to Marilla. "It's too bad there was a mistake with the orphan. Couldn't you have sent her back?"

"Well, we decided not to," Marilla explained. "Matthew took a fancy to her, and I must say I like her. She has her faults, but the house seems a different place already. She's a bright little thing."

"It's a big responsibility you've taken on," replied Mrs. Lynde, "especially since you've never had any experience with children. But I don't want to discourage you."

Anne was called inside. She did look a little odd in her dress that was too small and her hair that had been tussled by the wind.

"Well, they didn't pick you for your looks, that's certain," said Mrs. Lynde. "She's terrible skinny and homely, Marilla. Did anyone see such freckles? And hair as red as carrots!"

With one leap, Anne crossed the floor to Mrs. Lynde. "I hate you!" she cried in a choked voice, stamping her foot on the floor. "How dare you call me skinny and ugly? How dare you say I'm freckled and redheaded? You are a rude, unfeeling woman!"

"Anne!" exclaimed Marilla.

But Anne continued to face Mrs. Lynde with her hands clenched. "How would you like it if I said you were fat and clumsy? I don't care if I hurt your feelings by saying so! You have hurt mine worse than ever. I'll never forgive you. Never!"

"Did anybody ever see such a temper!" cried the horrified Mrs. Lynde.

"Anne, go to your room," Marilla said when she finally found her words. Anne burst into tears, ran off, and slammed the door.

"Well, I don't envy you bringing her up!" said Mrs. Lynde.

Marilla opened her mouth to apologize, but what came out instead was something different. "You shouldn't have said that about her looks, Rachel."

"Marilla Cuthbert, do you mean to say that you are

defending her terrible temper?" asked Mrs. Lynde.

"No," said Marilla slowly. "I'm not trying to excuse her. She's been very naughty, and I will punish her. But we must make allowances for Anne. She's never been taught what is right. And you *were* too hard on her, Rachel."

Mrs. Lynde got up, offended. "Well, I'll have to be careful what I say," she said. "I'm not angry—don't worry yourself. I'm too sorry for you. You'll have your troubles with that child. I guess her hair matches her temper. You can't expect me to visit here again in a hurry, if I'm liable to be insulted. Good evening." And she left.

Marilla went up to the east gable and found Anne facedown on her bed, crying bitterly.

"Anne," Marilla said gently. But there was no reply. "Anne, get up this minute and listen to what I have to say to you." Anne sat up and fixed her eyes on the floor. "This is a terrible way to behave, Anne! Aren't you ashamed of yourself?"

"She hadn't any right to call me ugly and red-headed," she said.

"You hadn't any right to fly into such a fury, Anne," said Marilla. "I wanted you to behave nicely to Mrs. Lynde, and instead you disgraced me. Mrs. Lynde will have a nice story to tell about you—everywhere."

"Just imagine how you would feel if somebody told

you that you were skinny and ugly," pleaded Anne tearfully.

Marilla suddenly remembered when she was a small child and heard someone say about her, "What a pity she is so homely." Marilla was almost fifty years old before that memory had stopped hurting.

"I don't think that Mrs. Lynde was exactly right in saying what she did, Anne," Marilla admitted in a softer tone, "but that is no excuse. You must tell her you are sorry and ask for her forgiveness."

"Oh, I can never do that," Anne said stubbornly. "You can punish me any way you like, but I cannot apologize to Mrs. Lynde."

"Then you'll stay here in your room until you can," replied Marilla.

"I shall stay here forever, then," Anne said mournfully. "I can't tell Mrs. Lynde that because I'm *not* sorry. I'm sorry I hurt you, but I'm glad I told her what I did."

"Perhaps you will change your mind by tomorrow morning," said Marilla. "You said you would try to be a good girl if we kept you, but I must say it hasn't seemed much like it this evening."

Marilla went down to the kitchen, quite troubled by what happened. She was just as angry with herself, though. Because whenever Marilla thought of Mrs. Lynde's surprised face at hearing Anne's words, she felt the most shameful urge to laugh.

~ 9 ~
Anne Apologizes

Marilla told Matthew what had happened that evening. "Well, it's a good thing Rachel Lynde got a talking to," Matthew said. "She sticks her nose into everybody's business."

Breakfast, lunch, and dinner were very quiet meals. Anne stayed in her room, refusing to give in. When Marilla went out that next evening to bring in the cows, Matthew crept inside the house.

He tiptoed to Anne's room. When he opened the door, he found her gazing sadly out the window. Matthew's heart ached for the little girl.

"Anne," he whispered, "how are you getting along?"

Anne forced a smile. "Alright. It's rather lonesome."

"Well now, Anne. Don't you think you'd better apologize and get it over with?" Matthew asked. "Marilla's a dreadful determined woman. It will have to be done sooner or later."

"I suppose I could for you," Anne said. "I *am* truly sorry now. I had decided to stay up here, but I'd apologize if you want me to."

"Well, of course I do, Anne," Matthew said. "It's terrible lonesome downstairs without you."

"Very well," said Anne. "I'll tell Marilla."

"Just don't tell Marilla I said anything. She might think I'm interfering, and I promised not to do that."

"Oh, I won't," she replied.

When Marilla returned from the cows, Anne told her that she would apologize to Mrs. Lynde. But on the way to see their neighbor, Anne did not look sorry at all. She walked with a light step and actually glowed. Marilla noted that something in her punishment was going wrong.

Anne's upbeat behavior continued until they stood in front of Mrs. Lynde. Before a word was spoken, Anne dropped to her knees and held out her hands.

"Oh, Mrs. Lynde, I am so extremely sorry," she said with a quiver in her voice. "I have behaved terribly to you—and I've disgraced my dear friends Matthew and Marilla, who have let me stay at Green Gables even though I'm not a boy. It was very wicked of me to fly into a temper because you told me the truth. What I said to you was true, too, but I shouldn't have said it. Oh, Mrs. Lynde, please, please forgive me. If you refuse, it will be a lifelong sadness to me. You wouldn't want to bring a lifelong sadness to a poor little orphan girl, would you?" Then Anne bowed her head and waited.

Mrs. Lynde was quite surprised, but she was

convinced that Anne was sincere. However, Marilla noticed that Anne was actually enjoying herself.

Luckily, Mrs. Lynde did not see this at all. Her face softened. "There, there, you may get up, child," she said. "Of course I forgive you. And I guess I was a little too hard on you, anyway."

"Oh, Mrs. Lynde, thank you," Anne replied.

"You can go to the garden and play now," Mrs. Lynde said.

When Anne had left, Mrs. Lynde turned to Marilla. "She's an odd little thing, but I'm not surprised you and Matthew decided to keep her. I kind of like her."

"I apologized pretty well, didn't I?" Anne asked Marilla on the walk home. "I thought since I had to do it, I might as well do it thoroughly."

"You did it thoroughly all right," Marilla agreed. She tried to hold back a laugh as she thought of Anne's apology.

"I have no hard feelings against Mrs. Lynde," Anne reported. "It gives you a nice feeling when you apologize and are forgiven."

Ahead they could just see the glow from the kitchen light at Green Gables. Anne suddenly came close to Marilla and slipped her hand into the older woman's palm. "It's lovely to go home and know it's home,"

Anne said. Something warm welled up in Marilla's heart at the touch of that little hand in her own. But its sweetness troubled her. *Perhaps it's simply a throb of motherly love I have missed all my life,* she thought.

~ 10 ~
A Promise

"Well, how do you like them?" Marilla asked. Anne was looking at three new dresses that Marilla had made spread out on the bed. One was a brown gingham, another was black-and-white checked, and the other was a stiff, ugly blue.

"I imagine that I like them," Anne said honestly.

"I don't want you to imagine it!" Marilla exclaimed.

"But they're—not pretty," Anne said.

"Pretty!" Marilla sniffed. "These are good, sensible dresses and they're all you'll get for now. I should think you'd be grateful not to wear your dress from the orphanage that is much too small."

"Oh, I am," Anne said quietly. "But I'd be ever so much *gratefuller* if I had one with puffed sleeves."

"I hadn't any extra material for puffed sleeves," Marilla said.

A week later, Marilla told Anne that she needed to see Mrs. Barry about a skirt pattern. If Anne wished, she could go along.

Anne clasped her hands and had tears on her face. "Oh, Marilla, what if Diana Barry doesn't like me!

It would the most *tragical* disappointment of my life!"

"Now, now," said Marilla. "I think Diana will like you well enough. It's her mother you need to worry about. You must be polite and well behaved, and don't make any of your startling speeches."

Marilla and Anne went to the Barry house, which was called Orchard Slope. When they arrived, Mrs. Barry greeted Marilla kindly. "And this must be the little girl you adopted?" she asked.

"Yes, this is Anne Shirley," replied Marilla.

"Spelled with an *e*," gasped Anne nervously.

"How are you?" Mrs. Barry asked.

"I am well in body although somewhat rumpled in spirit, thank you, ma'am," said Anne. Then she leaned over and whispered to Marilla, "That wasn't startling, was it, Marilla?"

Diana was a very pretty little girl with black hair. Once the girls were introduced, Mrs. Barry suggested they play in the garden. There Anne and Diana stood, gazing at each other shyly.

"Oh, Diana," Anne said at last. "Do you think you can like me a little—enough to be my bosom friend?"

Diana laughed. "Well, I guess so. I'm awfully glad you've come to Green Gables. It will be fun to have someone to play with."

"Will you swear to be my friend for ever and ever?" asked Anne eagerly. Diana agreed.

"We must join hands," said Anne in a serious tone. "I'll say the oath first: 'I solemnly swear to be faithful to my bosom friend, Diana Barry, as long as the sun and the moon shall endure.'"

Diana repeated the oath. Then she said, "You're a strange girl, Anne. But I'm going to like you real well."

When Marilla and Anne went home, Diana walked them as far as the bridge. The two girls had their arms around each other and promised to spend the next afternoon together.

"Well, did you find Diana a kindred spirit?" asked Marilla once they were home.

"Oh, yes," sighed Anne. "I'm the happiest girl on Prince Edward Island this very moment."

Though it seemed to Anne that she could not be any happier, Matthew arrived home with a surprise. He shyly pulled out a small package and handed it to Anne. "I heard you say you liked chocolate," he said.

"Humph," sniffed Marilla. "It'll ruin her teeth. There, there, child, don't look so sad. You can eat them, since Matthew got them. Just don't eat them all at once."

"Oh, I'll eat just one tonight," said Anne with a smile, "and I can give Diana half of them. I'm glad I have something for her."

When Anne had gone to her room, Marilla said to Matthew, "It's only been three weeks since Anne came, and it seems as if she has been here always. I can't imagine the place without her. Now don't give me that look of I-told-you-so, Matthew."

~ 11 ~
School Starts

W hen Anne started school in September, she and Diana walked there together. The girls got to sit next to each other by the window. Although Anne was behind in her studies from missing so much school, it didn't seem to bother her.

"I think I'm going to like school here," Anne had told Marilla the first day. "Ruby Gillis gave me an apple, and Tillie Boulter let me wear her bead ring, and Jane Andrews said I had a pretty nose. That is the first compliment I have ever had." Indeed Anne liked most things about school except for her teacher, Mr. Phillips.

Three weeks into school, Diana and Anne were walking on the Birch Path, a lovely walking path through a forest of birch trees that Anne had named herself. "I guess Gilbert Blythe will be in school today," said Diana. "He's been away all summer and just got home. He's awfully handsome. And he teases the girls something terrible." By the way Diana said this, she didn't seem to mind Gilbert Blythe's teasing.

That day Gilbert Blythe was sitting across the aisle from Anne. He was a tall boy with curly hair and a teasing smile. He was pinning Ruby Gillis's braid to the back of her seat. When Ruby tried to get up, she fell back in her seat with a shriek. Mr. Phillips glared at Ruby while Gilbert pretended to study history. Then he winked at Anne.

"I think Gilbert Blythe is handsome," Anne said to Diana. "But it's bad manners to wink at a strange girl."

Later that afternoon, Anne was staring dreamily out of the window at the Lake of Shining Waters. She didn't notice that Gilbert Blythe was trying to get her attention. And he wasn't used to girls not noticing him. He tried again but failed. Almost desperate, Gilbert picked up the end of Anne's braid and said in a loud whisper, "Carrots! Carrots!"

Anne sprang to her feet in anger. "You mean, hateful boy!" she shouted. Then she raised her slate over her head and—*thwack!* Anne brought her slate down on Gilbert's head. The slate cracked in two.

The students said, "Oh!" in surprise. Diana gasped. Mr. Phillips marched down the aisle and laid his hand heavily on Anne's shoulder. "Anne Shirley, what does this mean?" he asked angrily.

"It was my fault, Mr. Phillips. I teased her," Gilbert spoke up.

Mr. Phillips did not pay attention to Gilbert. "I am sorry a student of mine is showing such temper," he said. "Anne, go stand in front of the blackboard for the rest of the day."

Anne's anger at Gilbert Blythe got her through her embarrassment that day. She would not look at him. She would never look at or speak to Gilbert Blythe again!

When school was over, Anne marched out with her head held high. Gilbert walked up to her on the porch. "I'm awful sorry I made fun of your hair, Anne," he said. "Don't be mad for keeps now."

Anne walked right past him.

"Oh, how could you, Anne?" Diana asked as they walked home. Diana felt that she could never have resisted Gilbert's apology. "You mustn't mind Gilbert," she said. "He makes fun of all the girls. I've never heard him apologize before, either."

"I shall never forgive him," Anne said firmly.

The next day Mr. Phillips announced children could no longer come in late after lunch. When he returned from lunch, everyone should be in his or her seat. Those who were late would be punished.

Many children went to the spruce grove as usual at lunchtime. When they saw their teacher walking back to school, the girls were on the ground running. The boys were in the trees, so they arrived later. And Anne, who was daydreaming, was latest of all. Anne could run like a deer, though, and she passed the boys and arrived in the schoolhouse just in front of them.

Mr. Phillips was hanging his hat. He didn't want to

punish all twelve students, but he needed to keep his word. "Anne Shirley, since you seem to like the boys, go and sit with Gilbert Blythe."

The boys snickered. Diana turned pale and squeezed Anne's hand. Anne sat down beside Gilbert. She buried her face in her arms on the desk. This was the end. It was bad enough to be the only person punished among twelve guilty ones. But to be made to sit with a boy— Gilbert Blythe of all boys—she couldn't bear it.

Anne did not lift her head from her desk the rest of the day. When school was over, Anne marched to her desk and took everything out of it.

"Why are you taking all of that?" asked Diana on the road home.

"I'm not coming back to school," Anne said.

"Oh, Anne," cried Diana. "What will I do? Mr. Phillips will make me sit next to Gertie Pye. Please come back."

"I'd do almost anything in the world for you, Diana," Anne said sadly. "But I can't do this, so please don't ask."

Since Marilla could see how stubborn Anne was about not returning to school, she did not try to reason with her that afternoon. Instead she went to see Mrs. Lynde and ask her advice.

Of course, Mrs. Lynde had already heard what had happened. "I think Mr. Phillips was in the wrong,"

Mrs. Lynde said. "The others who were late should have been punished as well. I would let Anne stay home for now."

"You really think so?" Marilla asked.

"Yes. I wouldn't say anything about going back until Anne does herself. She'll cool off in a week or so."

Marilla took Mrs. Lynde's advice. Anne learned her schoolwork at home and did her chores. Anne insisted that she would hate Gilbert Blythe until the end of her life.

Although Anne's young heart could hate, she could love fiercely also. And she loved Diana. One evening Marilla found Anne crying bitterly in her room.

"What's the matter, Anne?" she asked.

"It's about Diana," sobbed Anne. "I love her so. But when we grow up, Diana will get married and leave me. I've been imagining it—Diana dressed in a white dress with a veil, looking like a queen. And I am a bridesmaid wearing puffed sleeves, with a smile on my face, but with a heart that is breaking inside—" Anne sobbed harder.

Marilla turned away but could not hide her smile. She collapsed in a chair and burst into laughter. Matthew heard her in the yard and stood in amazement. *When had Marilla laughed like that?*

"Well, Anne Shirley," Marilla said as soon as she could speak. "You sure do have an imagination."

~ 12 ~

Diana Is Invited to Tea

In October, Anne invited Diana to tea. Marilla was to be gone that day, so the girls would have their very own grown-up visit.

"You can open the cherry preserves, Anne," offered Marilla. "And put out some fruitcake and cookies. There's a bottle of raspberry cordial on the second shelf for you two as well."

Diana arrived dressed in her second-best dress and knocked on the door formally. The girls shook hands as if they had never met. They went to the sitting room and asked politely about each other's families, and then Diana told Anne all that was going on in school. Since Anne had left, Diana had to sit next to Gertie Pye, which she didn't like at all. Everybody missed Anne, Diana said.

When it was time for tea, Anne told Diana about the special raspberry cordial. She found it on the shelf and put the bottle on the table with a large glass.

"Now please help yourself, Diana," Anne said politely. "I'm too full from eating apples to have some just yet."

Diana poured herself a large glassful and admired

44

its lovely red color. "It's awfully nice raspberry cordial, Anne," she said. "It's the nicest I ever drank, and it doesn't taste a bit like Mrs. Lynde's."

Anne went to set up their tea. When she returned, Diana was on her second large glass of cordial. While Anne talked on and on, Diana poured and drank a third glass. Suddenly Diana stood up unsteadily.

"I'm awful sick," she said. "I must go home right away."

"But we haven't had tea yet. You can't leave now," said Anne.

"I must go home," Diana said again. "I'm awful dizzy."

And indeed she walked very dizzily. With tears of disappointment in her eyes, Anne got Diana's hat and walked her to the end of the yard. Anne cried all the way back to the house.

The next afternoon Marilla sent Anne to Mrs. Lynde's on an errand. A little while later, Anne came running back and flung herself on the kitchen sofa, crying loudly.

"Whatever has gone wrong now, Anne?" asked Marilla.

"Mrs. Lynde said Mrs. Barry is terribly upset," she wailed. "She says I got Diana drunk yesterday. She says she's never going to let Diana play with me again!"

Marilla stared in amazement. "Drunk!" she said

when she found her voice. "Anne, what on earth did you give her?"

"Raspberry cordial," Anne replied. "She liked it so much she had three large glasses full."

"That's ridiculous," cried Marilla, marching to the cupboard. But there on the shelf was a bottle of red currant wine. Now Marilla remembered that she had left the raspberry cordial down in the cellar instead of in the cupboard as she had told Anne.

"Anne, you certainly have a gift for getting into trouble." Marilla sighed. "You gave Diana currant wine instead of raspberry cordial. Now, don't cry. You are not to blame. It was an accident."

"My heart is broken," Anne said. "We are parted forever."

"Don't be silly," said Marilla. "Mrs. Barry will understand when she finds out you didn't do it on purpose. I'll go up this evening and tell her what happened."

But when Marilla got back, she could not say it was going to be all right. "What an unreasonable woman!" snapped Marilla. "Mrs. Barry didn't believe that it was a mistake."

Anne could not wait a moment longer. She flew out the door and over the fields to the Barrys' house. Mrs. Barry answered the door with a hardened face. "What do you want?" she said stiffly.

46

Anne clasped her hands and asked for forgiveness for her mistake. But Anne's apology did not change Mrs. Barry's mind.

"I don't think you are a fit little girl for Diana to play with. You'd better go home now and behave."

Anne went back to Green Gables with a heavy heart. "My last hope is gone. Mrs. Barry treated me very insultingly, Marilla. I do *not* think she is such a good woman."

"Anne, you shouldn't say such things," said Marilla. She was trying hard to hold back the laughter that was about to come out. Anne was right, and Marilla was amused at the situations Anne got herself into.

But when Marilla came to Anne's room before she went to bed, she could see that Anne had cried herself to sleep. "Poor little soul," Marilla whispered. Then she bent down and kissed Anne's red cheek.

~ 13 ~
A New Interest

Anne looked out the kitchen window the next day and saw Diana waving at her. "Has your mother changed her mind?" Anne asked breathlessly when she arrived outside.

"No," said Diana miserably. "She said I was never to play with you again. I cried and cried and told her it wasn't your fault, but she wouldn't listen. I've come to say good-bye."

"Diana, will you promise never to forget me?" Anne asked.

"Indeed, I will," said Diana. "I will never have another bosom friend. I couldn't love anybody as I love you."

"I didn't know you loved me!" cried Anne. "I didn't think anybody could love me. Oh, this is a ray of light in the darkness. And I will always love thee. Wilt thou give me a lock of thy hair for a parting treasure?"

Diana nodded.

Anne clipped one of Diana's curls. "Farewell, my beloved friend. My heart will always be with thee." Anne stood and watched miserably as Diana walked away.

"I shall never have another friend," Anne said to

Marilla when she went inside. "Diana and I had a romantic farewell. I used the most tragic language I could think of and said 'thou' and 'thee.' I'm going to wear Diana's lock of hair in a pouch around my neck all my life. Please see that it is buried with me. I don't believe I'll live very long."

"I don't think there is much fear of you dying of grief as long as you can talk, Anne," Marilla replied.

The following Monday Anne surprised Marilla by announcing that she was going back to school. "It's all I have left," she said. "At least at school I can gaze at Diana and think of our friendship."

When Anne went back to school she was heartily welcomed. That afternoon a note and a small package were passed to Anne.

Dear Anne,
Mother says I'm not to play with you or talk to you even in school. I love you as much as ever. I made you a new bookmark. When you look at it, remember your true friend,
Diana Barry

Anne read the note and wrote back.

Darling Diana,
Of course I'm not cross with you because you have to obey your mother. I shall keep your lovely present forever.
Yours until death do us part,
Anne or Cordelia Shirley

Marilla expected more trouble from Anne, but none came. Anne got along well with Mr. Phillips now, and she flung herself into her studies. She still would not speak to Gilbert Blythe, or even look in his direction. And she was determined that he would not get ahead of her in school. At the end of each month, written tests were given. The first month, Gilbert was ahead of Anne by three points; the next month, Anne had beaten him by five.

By the end of the term, they began studying harder subjects—the toughest for Anne was geometry. "I'm not sure I can ever understand this," Anne told Marilla. "Mr. Phillips thinks I'm a dunce at it. Diana does very well in geometry, but I don't mind being beaten by her." Anne studied harder than ever to keep ahead of Gilbert Blythe.

Anne to the Rescue

On a January evening Marilla and most of the townspeople went to Charlottetown to hear the Canadian premier speak. The trip was about thirty miles away. Matthew stayed home with Anne that evening while she struggled with geometry.

"Well, you do just fine at anything, Anne," Matthew said. "Mr. Phillips told me that you was the smartest student in school."

They heard the sound of quick footsteps on the porch, and the door was flung open. Diana stood there, breathless and white-faced.

"Whatever is the matter?" cried Anne.

"Come quick," said Diana. "Minnie May is awful sick—she's got croup. Mother and Father are in town and there's no one to go for the doctor. Mary Joe doesn't know what to do—and I'm so scared!"

Matthew reached for his coat without a word and walked past Diana into the yard. "He's gone to harness the horse and go for the doctor," Anne said.

Diana started to cry. "Don't worry," Anne said. "I know exactly what to do for croup. Mrs. Hammond's twins had croup regularly. I'll get the ipecac bottle."

The two girls ran hand in hand toward Diana's house in the deep snow. Three-year-old Minnie May was very sick indeed. She lay on the sofa feverish and restless. Her hoarse breathing could be heard all over the house. Young Mary Joe had been hired to watch the children, but she knew nothing about croup.

Anne took charge. "Minnie May is pretty bad, but I've seen worse. First, we need lots of hot water. Diana, find some soft cloths. I'm going to give her the ipecac syrup."

Anne gave Minnie Mae the medicine several times throughout the long night. She and Diana worked patiently over the poor child. It was three o'clock in the morning when Matthew came with the doctor. He had to go all the way to Spencervale to find one. But the desperate need for the doctor had passed. Minnie May was much better and was now sleeping soundly.

"I was almost ready to give up," Anne explained to the doctor. "She got worse until she was sicker than the twins ever were. I thought she was going to choke to death. I gave her the last drop of ipecac, and I knew it was the only hope we had. After a bit, she got better. I was so relieved that I just can't express it in words."

"I understand," the doctor said.

Later the doctor spoke with Mr. and Mrs. Barry about Anne. "That redheaded girl is as smart as they make them. She saved that baby's life, for it would have been too late by the time I got here."

Matthew took Anne home on a wonderful snowy winter morning. She fell into bed and slept until the next afternoon. Marilla had a large breakfast waiting for Anne when she got up. "Matthew has been telling me about last night," she said. "It was a good thing you knew what to do, Anne. I wouldn't have."

Marilla had something to tell Anne. "Mrs. Barry was here this afternoon. She said you saved Minnie May's life, and she is sorry for the way she acted toward you. She knows now you didn't do anything to hurt Diana on purpose. And she hopes you'll forgive her and be friends with Diana again. You can go over if you like—now, Anne Shirley, don't fly clear up into the air!"

But nothing could hold Anne down. "Oh, Marilla, can I go right now without washing my dishes?"

"Yes, yes, run along," Marilla said.

Anne didn't wait to hear more. She raced out the front door.

Anne came home that evening in a dreamy state. "I am now a perfectly happy person, Marilla," she said. "Yes, in spite of my red hair. Mrs. Barry kissed me and cried and said she was so sorry. She had an elegant tea on her best china. No one has *ever* used china for me. It must be lovely to be a grown-up—just being treated like one is nice."

~ 15 ~
A Concert

Diana signaled Anne from her window to come out right away. She was bursting with excitement. For her birthday, Diana was inviting Anne to go to a concert in town and then spend the night.

The next day they had tea at Diana's. Anne felt embarrassed by her plain, tight-sleeved dress, but she used her imagination and was able to pretend she was in a much lovelier dress.

The program that night was one thrill after another for Anne. Many people recited, including their teacher and children from school. But when Gilbert Blythe recited, Anne read her book until he was finished. She did not clap.

"Anne, how could you pretend not to listen to him?" Diana asked. "He looked right at you." Anne did not want to discuss it.

When the girls were back at Diana's house, they decided to race to see who could get into pajamas first. They were so excited to be allowed to sleep in the spare bedroom, a room used only for special guests.

The girls bounded out Diana's bedroom door

toward the spare bedroom. They jumped into the bed at the same time. And then—something moved beneath them! There was a gasp and a cry.

Anne and Diana nearly flew out of the room and back down the hall. "Who—what was that?" whispered Anne in a scared tone.

"It was Aunt Josephine," said Diana, gasping with laughter. "I didn't know she would be here tonight. Oh, she will be furious. But it *is* funny."

At breakfast, Diana and Anne ate quickly before Aunt Josephine got up. Later that day, Mrs. Lynde said she had seen Mrs. Barry, who was very upset. The old aunt wouldn't speak to Diana at all. Aunt Josephine had planned to stay for a month, but now she decided she wouldn't stay another day. Aunt Josephine was a rich and generous aunt, and the Barrys had always treated her very well.

Anne felt terrible. When she arrived at Orchard Slope, Diana met her at the door. Anne didn't want Diana to take all of the blame. It had been her idea to race to the spare bedroom.

"I'm going in to tell Miss Barry what happened," said Anne.

"Anne, you can't do that! She'll eat you alive!" cried Diana.

"It was my fault, and I've got to confess," said Anne.

So Anne entered the sitting room. Miss Josephine

Barry was sitting up straight and she wheeled around in her chair. "Who are you?" she asked.

"I'm Anne of Green Gables," Anne answered in a trembling voice. Anne explained how the girls were just having fun and that she should be angry with Anne instead of Diana. "I'm so used to having people cross at me that I can endure it much better than Diana can."

The old woman's eyes seemed to twinkle with interest, but she said coldly, "Little girls were never allowed that kind of fun when I was young. You don't know what it's like to be awakened like that."

"I don't know, but I can imagine," said Anne. "If you have an imagination, think of yourself in our place. We were so excited to sleep in the spare bedroom. I suppose you are used to sleeping in spare bedrooms, but for a little orphan girl it is such an honor."

Miss Barry let out a hearty laugh. "I'm afraid my imagination is a little rusty," Miss Barry answered. "Sit and tell me about yourself."

Anne stayed to talk and told Miss Barry about Marilla bringing her up. She asked again if Diana could be forgiven and if Miss Barry could stay in Avonlea as originally planned.

"I think I will stay if you will come over and talk to me occasionally," Miss Barry said.

That evening Aunt Josephine unpacked her bag. "I want to get to know that Anne-girl. She amuses me, and, at my age, amusement is hard to find."

Over the next month, Anne and Miss Barry became fast friends. Before Miss Barry left town, she told Anne she could sleep in her spare bedroom any time she visited.

~ 16 ~

A Test of Anne's Honor

In June the people of Avonlea learned they were to lose their schoolteacher, Mr. Phillips, as well as their minister. A new minister, Mr. Allan, had moved into town.

Anne loved the minister's wife, Mrs. Allan, with all her heart. She had found another kindred spirit. Mrs. Allan taught Anne's Sunday school class and allowed her students to ask as many questions as they wanted. Anne could not have been happier.

One day Anne came dancing up the lane after a trip to the post office. She wore her excitement like a coat around her. "I am invited to tea at Mrs. Allan's house tomorrow!" she said to Marilla.

"Do learn to take things calmly, Anne," Marilla responded.

But it wasn't Anne's nature to take things calmly. Although Marilla appeared to want Anne to be a quiet young girl with perfect manners, Marilla secretly liked Anne just the way she was.

Through that night, Anne was worried that she wouldn't behave properly at Mrs. Allan's house. When

Anne returned home after tea the next day, she told Marilla all about it.

"I had a most fascinating time," she said. "You know, there are some people, like Matthew and Mrs. Allan, whom you can love right off, without any trouble. And there are other people, like Mrs. Lynde, whom you have to try very hard to love. Mrs. Allan and I had a heart-to-heart talk. I told her everything about the asylum and coming to Green Gables and geometry. And would you believe it? Mrs. Allan said she was a dunce at geometry, too. Then Mrs. Allan said she had heard that a new teacher had been hired. Her name is Miss Muriel Stacy. I can hardly wait until school begins."

Almost a month had passed since Anne had been in any trouble. So it was high time something went wrong.

Before school started, Diana was having a party with all the girls in her class. The girls played in the garden after their tea and dared each other to do things.

Someone dared Josie Pye to walk along the top of the board fence. Josie completed her task and seemed proud of herself.

"I knew a girl who walked a ridgepole on a roof," Anne said.

"I don't believe it," said Josie. "No one could walk a ridgepole—you couldn't anyway."

"Couldn't I?" Anne said without thinking.

"Then I dare you to walk the ridgepole on this roof," said Josie.

Anne turned pale, but there was only one thing to do.

"Don't do it, Anne," begged Diana. "You'll fall off and be killed. Never mind Josie Pye."

"My honor is at stake," said Anne bravely. "I shall walk the ridgepole, Diana, or die trying. If I am killed you can have my pearl bead ring."

Anne climbed the ladder amidst the girls' breathless silence. She got on the ridgepole, balanced herself, and started to walk. Anne was aware that she was very high up. She managed to take several steps before the disaster came. She swayed, stumbled, lost her balance, and slid down the roof, crashing into the bushes.

If Anne had fallen off the other side, Diana would have gotten Anne's pearl ring. Luckily, the side she fell on was closer to the ground. The girls ran to Anne. They found her lying limp on the ground.

"Anne, are you killed?" shrieked Diana. She threw herself on the ground next to her friend. "Oh, Anne, dear Anne, just speak one word!"

To everyone's great relief, Anne spoke. "No, Diana, I am not killed, but I think I am unconscious."

Then Mrs. Barry appeared. "Where are you hurt?" she asked.

"My ankle," gasped Anne.

Marilla was out in the orchard when she saw Mr. Barry coming up the hill carrying Anne, who was lying limp in his arms. Mrs. Barry walked beside him, and a line of girls was following.

Marilla felt a sudden stab of fear. She realized right then what Anne had come to mean to her. As Marilla hurried wildly down the hill, she knew that she loved Anne more than anything on earth.

"Mr. Barry, what has happened?" Marilla gasped.

Anne lifted her head. "Don't be frightened. I was walking along the ridgepole and fell off. I think I've sprained my ankle." Then Anne's head fell back.

"Mercy me, the child has fainted!" said Marilla. Anne was overcome by the pain. The doctor said Anne had broken her ankle.

"Aren't you very sorry for me?" Anne asked Marilla that night.

"It was your own fault," Marilla responded.

"I just couldn't turn down Josie Pye's dare," Anne said. "I've been punished enough with this ankle, so you don't need to be angry with me, Marilla. I can't go to school for seven weeks. I'll miss meeting the new teacher. And Gil—everybody will get ahead of me in school."

"There, there, I'm not cross," said Marilla.

Anne had many visitors. Mrs. Allan came often and

Diana visited every day. "Diana tells me exciting things about the new teacher," Anne said. "The girls think Miss Stacy is perfectly sweet."

"One thing is certain," Marilla said. "Your tongue wasn't hurt at all."

~ 17 ~
The Students' Concert

It was October when Anne was ready to return to school. It was wonderful to be back at the little brown desk next to Diana.

Miss Stacy was a bright young woman. Anne found her to be another true and helpful friend. Under her teaching, Anne blossomed like a flower. "I love Miss Stacy," Anne said. "When she says my name, I feel she is spelling it with an *e*."

Miss Stacy was planning for the Avonlea school to present a concert Christmas night. The concert would raise money for a new flag for their school. No one was quite as excited as Anne Shirley.

Marilla thought it foolish. "It's just filling your heads up with nonsense and taking time away from schoolwork," she said.

But Anne did not pay much attention to Marilla's comments. She was just too excited. "We're going to have six choruses, and Diana is singing a solo. I will have two recitations. Don't you hope your little Anne does well?"

"I just hope you behave yourself," Marilla replied. "When all this fuss is over, I hope you can settle down.

You are good for nothing right now. It's a wonder your tongue is not worn out."

Anne sighed and went out in the backyard to find Matthew. He was splitting wood. Anne sat and talked about the concert with him. He was always a sympathetic listener.

"Well, I expect you'll do your part fine," he said to Anne. He smiled at her eager little face. Anne smiled back at him. Matthew and Anne were the best of friends, and Matthew was thankful he did not have to discipline Anne. He was free to "spoil" her, as Marilla called it. And it was not a bad arrangement. A little spoiling sometimes did as much good as all the careful discipline in the world.

~ 18 ~

Matthew Insists on Puffed Sleeves

On a December evening Matthew hid in the kitchen while Anne and her school friends were practicing for the concert. He was too shy to say hello. Matthew peeked out to see bright-eyed Anne among her friends. But he noticed that something about Anne was different from the other girls.

After thinking about it for several hours, he knew what it was. Anne was not dressed like the others! Marilla kept Anne in such plain clothes. Matthew did not know anything about fashion, but he was sure that Anne's sleeves looked different than the others, too.

Maybe it would be all right to let the child have one pretty dress—like the ones Diana always wore. So Matthew decided that he would give Anne a dress. Christmas was only two weeks away.

The very next evening, Matthew went to buy the material for the dress. He decided to go to Lawson's store because he thought there were no female sales clerks he'd have to talk to. But when he arrived, a woman was behind the counter. Matthew got so flustered that he left with a garden rake and brown sugar, but no material.

Mathew decided that a woman was needed. Since he knew Marilla would not approve, he went to Mrs. Lynde. "Pick out a dress for you to give to Anne?" she asked. "Of course I will. I'm going to Carmody tomorrow. Would you like me to make the dress since Anne might see it if Marilla made it? It wouldn't be any trouble."

"Yes, thank you. I'm much obliged," Matthew answered. "And—I think they make the sleeves different nowadays. If it wouldn't be too much to ask—I'd like them made in the new way."

"Puffs? Of course. You needn't worry a speck more about it, Matthew. I'll make it up in the latest fashion." Once Matthew left, Mrs. Lynde thought to herself. *It will be good to see that poor child wearing something decent. The way Marilla dresses her is ridiculous. I've ached to tell her. I'm sure Anne feels her clothes are different from all the other girls. And to think Matthew noticed it!*

On Christmas Eve, Mrs. Lynde brought up the new dress. *So this is what Matthew has been grinning about for the past two weeks*, Marilla thought to herself.

"Well, I don't think Anne needed any new dresses,"

Marilla said. "I hope she'll be satisfied now because I know she's been longing for these silly sleeves for the past few years."

Christmas morning broke on a beautiful white world. Anne ran downstairs singing. "Merry Christmas, Marilla! Merry Christmas, Matthew! Isn't it lovely? Why—why—Matthew, is that for me?"

He had sheepishly unfolded the dress from its paper and held it out. Marilla pretended to fill the teapot, but watched Anne and Matthew out of the corner of her eye.

Anne looked at the dress in awe. She did not say a word. How pretty it was, with the silky material, a skirt with frills, and a pin-tucked waist. And the sleeves! Long puffs with bows of silk ribbon.

"That's a Christmas present for you, Anne," said Matthew shyly. "Why—Anne, don't you like it?"

Anne's eyes had suddenly filled with tears.

"Like it! Oh, Matthew! It's perfectly beautiful. I can never thank you enough. Look at those sleeves! Oh, I must be dreaming."

After breakfast Diana came to visit. Anne told her all about the dress. "I've got something for you," Diana said. "This box was sent to you from Aunt Josephine." Inside was a pair of little slippers with beaded toes and satin bows. Anne could hardly believe it.

"Now you won't have to borrow Ruby's slippers for

the concert," Diana said. "They are two sizes too big for you anyway."

That evening the concert went splendidly. The little hall was crowded, and all the performers did well. However, the star of the show was Anne. "Your recitations brought down the house, Anne," said Diana that night when they were walking home.

"Well, your solo was perfectly elegant, Diana," said Anne. "You didn't look nervous. I was so nervous I worried for a moment that I could not speak. Then I thought of my puffed sleeves and took courage. I knew I must live up to those sleeves."

"Wasn't the boys' dialogue fine?" said Diana. "Gilbert Blythe did wonderfully. Anne, I do think it's awful mean how you treat Gil. When you ran off the stage, one of the roses fell out of your hair. Gil picked it up and put it in his pocket. Isn't that romantic?"

"I don't care at all what that person does," Anne replied coolly.

After Anne had gone to bed that evening, Matthew and Marilla sat by the fire. They had just been to their first concert in twenty years. "Well, I guess our Anne did well tonight," Matthew said.

"Yes, she did," said Marilla. "She's a bright child. And she looked real nice, too. I was proud of Anne tonight, although I'm not going to tell her so."

"Well, I was proud of her, and I did tell her so,"

Matthew said. "I guess Anne will need something more than Avonlea School sometime soon. We must see what we can do for her."

"She's only thirteen in March," Marilla said. "Though tonight I noticed she is growing into a big girl. I guess the best thing for her will be to send her to Queen's, but nothing needs to be said yet."

~ 19 ~

Red Turned Green

Marilla was walking home one April night, thinking of the warm fire and tea that were waiting for her. Anne was to have it ready when she came home.

But when Marilla entered the kitchen, there was no fire and no sign of Anne. "I don't care if Mrs. Allan does say she's the brightest and sweetest child she ever knew," Marilla said to Matthew. "She's probably off playing somewhere."

It was dark when dinner was ready, and there was still no sign of Anne. Marilla went up to the east gable for a candle. She found Anne lying facedown on the bed.

"Mercy," gasped Marilla. "Are you sick, Anne?"

"No," came the muffled reply. Anne buried deeper into her pillow. "Please go away, Marilla, and don't look at me. I'll never be able to go anywhere again."

"Anne Shirley, what have you done?" Marilla demanded.

"Look at my hair, Marilla," she whispered.

Marilla lifted her candle to look. "Why, it's *green*!" It was a strange green color with streaks of the original red.

Never had Marilla seen hair quite so terrible looking.

"I thought nothing could be as bad as red hair," moaned Anne, "but this is ten times worse. I dyed it."

"Dyed it!" exclaimed Marilla.

"I thought it worth it to get rid of my red hair. I didn't mean to dye it green. The peddler whom I bought it from said it would turn my hair a beautiful raven black."

"See where your vanity has led you, Anne?" said Marilla. "I suppose the first thing is to give your hair a good washing and see if that helps."

But it did not. Anne scrubbed and scrubbed, but the dye did not wash out. "Oh, Marilla," wailed Anne. "I am the unhappiest girl in Prince Edward Island!"

Anne didn't go anywhere for a week. Finally, Marilla told her she must cut off her hair. There was no other way. When Anne returned to school, she was relieved that no one guessed the reason for her short hair.

"Josie Pye told me I looked like a scarecrow," Anne said to Marilla that evening. Marilla was lying on the couch after one of her headaches. "Am I talking too much? Does it hurt your head?"

"My head is better now, but it was terrible this afternoon," said Marilla. "These headaches are getting worse. As for your chatter, I don't really mind. I've gotten used to it."

~ 20 ~

An Unfortunate Lily Maid

O f course, you must be Elaine, Anne," said
Diana. "I don't have the courage to float down
the pond."

"But a red-haired person cannot be a lily maid,"
Anne said.

"Your hair is much darker than before you cut it.
And it's real pretty," Diana said, admiring the curls
clustering around Anne's head.

"Oh, do you think so?" exclaimed Anne, blushing
with delight.

Ruby, Jane, Diana, and Anne were standing on the
bank of the pond. They had decided to act out a scene
from a poem they had read in school. They found a raft
they could let drift with the current under the bridge.
It would stop at the headland farther down.

"Well, I guess I'll be Elaine," Anne said finally.
"Ruby, you must be King Arthur and Jane will be
Guinevere and Diana will be Lancelot." Anne lay down
with her eyes closed and her hands folded across her
chest. She was supposed to be dead in this scene.

"We must kiss her brow and say, 'Farewell forever, sweet sister' as sadly as we can," said Diana. "Now push off the raft."

Jane, Diana, and Ruby ran through the woods down to the headland where they would meet the raft with the lily maid. Anne drifted slowly down and was enjoying the romance of the ride. Then the raft began to leak. Anne scrambled to her feet and looked at the water pouring in. The raft was going to sink!

Anne gave a little scream that no one else could hear. She had one chance—just one. When the raft bumped into one of the pilings of the bridge, Anne scrambled up and hung on. But there was one problem. Anne could not get up or down. So she hung on tightly.

In the next moment, the raft sank farther downstream. The other girls saw it disappear and they thought Anne had gone down with it. They stood staring for a moment in disbelief and then ran shrieking up the hill through the woods. Unfortunately, they did not see Anne hanging on under the bridge.

Minutes passed. *Where have the girls gone?* Anne thought. *Suppose I grow so tired that I cannot hold on any longer?*

Just as Anne thought she would have to let go and fall to her death, a boat passed underneath the bridge. It was Gilbert Blythe! He looked up. "Anne Shirley!

How on earth did you get there?"

He pulled close and put out his hand. Taking it, Anne climbed down into the boat. She sat down, relieved but furious.

"What happened?" Gilbert asked.

"We were playing Elaine," she explained without even looking at her rescuer. "I had to drift down to Camelot on a raft. But it began to leak and the girls went for help. Will you be kind enough to row me to the dock?"

Once there, Anne jumped ashore. "I'm much obliged to you," she said coldly and turned to leave. But Gilbert jumped from the boat and laid a hand on her arm.

"Anne," he said hurriedly, "can't we be good friends? I'm awfully sorry I made fun of your hair. Besides, it was long ago. I think your hair is awfully pretty now."

For a moment, Anne waited. The shy, eager expression on Gilbert's face made her heart give a quick beat. But the anger of her old memories rose up. He had embarrassed her in front of the whole school. She would never forgive Gilbert Blythe!

"No," she said. "I shall never be friends with you."

"All right!" he responded and got in the boat to leave. "I'll never ask you again, Anne Shirley! And I don't care, either!"

Anne walked up the path with her head high. But she had a terrible feeling that she ought to have answered Gilbert differently. Halfway up the path, she met the girls rushing back to the pond in a frenzy. "Oh, Anne," gasped Diana with relief, falling into Anne's arms when she saw her. "We thought you had drowned. How did you escape?"

Anne told them what had happened. "Gilbert saved you. How romantic!" Jane said. "Of course, you'll speak to him now."

"Of course I won't," said Anne quickly. "I'm awfully sorry you were so frightened, girls."

Once Anne was safely back at home and she had told Marilla everything, she felt better. Anne had been so scared by her near drowning and humiliated by being saved by Gilbert Blythe. However, Marilla did not feel better.

"Will you ever have any sense, Anne?" Marilla groaned.

"Oh yes, I think I will," she said. "Since I arrived at Green Gables, I've made mistakes. And each mistake has cured me of one of my faults. The time I walked the ridgepole cured me of my pride; dyeing my hair cured me of my vanity; and today's mistake will cure me of being too romantic. I am quite sure you will see a big improvement in me soon."

"I sure hope so," Marilla replied.

Matthew had been listening. When Marilla left the room, he laid a hand on Anne's shoulder. "Don't lose all your romance, Anne," he whispered shyly. "A little bit of it is a good thing."

The Queen's Class
Is Organized

Marilla laid her knitting in her lap and sat back in her chair. Lately her eyes had grown tired often. Marilla looked over at Anne, who was sitting on the rug, daydreaming. She had learned to love this slim, gray-eyed girl immensely. But Anne had no idea how Marilla felt about her.

"Anne," said Marilla. "Miss Stacy was here this afternoon. She wants to organize a class of her advanced students to study for the Queen's entrance exam. She came to ask Matthew and me if you could join it. Would you like to go to Queen's and be a teacher, Anne?"

"Oh, Marilla!" Anne clasped her hands. "It's been my life's dream. But won't it be expensive?"

"You needn't worry about that," Marilla said. "When Matthew and I took you, we decided we would give you a good education. A girl should be able to earn her own living, whether or not she has to. You'll always have a home here at Green Gables. But it's good to be prepared. So you can join the Queen's class if you like, Anne."

"Thank you, Marilla!" she cried. Anne flung her arms around Marilla's waist and looked up into her face. "I'm very grateful to you and Matthew, and I'll study as hard as I can."

"You'll get along well enough. Miss Stacy says you are bright and you work hard." Marilla did not tell Anne all that Miss Stacy said about her. She feared it would make Anne think too much of herself. "You have about a year and a half before the exams, so you'll have plenty of time to get ready."

The class to study for the Queen's exam was organized. Gilbert Blythe, Anne Shirley, Ruby Gillis, Jane Andrews, and Josie Pye were all in it, but Diana was not. Being separated was very difficult for both girls.

But Anne soon found the class quite interesting. She had always wanted to be first in her class ahead of Gilbert Blythe, but now Gilbert wanted to be first as well. Since her rescue at the bridge, Gilbert had simply ignored Anne. Now Anne understood that being ignored was not at all pleasant. If she had the chance to answer Gilbert differently, Anne would have. She was not angry with Gilbert anymore and had forgiven him. But now it was too late.

The winter passed and Anne studied hard and was happy otherwise. Then spring came again to Green Gables. By the end of the school year in June, the students were less interested in their studies.

"You've all worked hard this year and you deserve a vacation," Miss Stacy told her class. "Have the best time you can outdoors this summer so that you are ready to study again in the fall—for the last year before the entrance exam."

When Anne got home that night, she piled her schoolbooks in the attic. "I'm not going to look at books this summer," she told Marilla. "I'm going to let my imagination run wild. I want to have fun this summer since it might be the last summer I am a little girl."

Mrs. Lynde came up the next day to see why Marilla wasn't at the Aid meeting. "Matthew had a bad spell with his heart, and I didn't want to leave him," Marilla explained. "The doctor says he cannot get excited, and he's not to do heavy work. You might as well tell Matthew not to breathe as not to work."

Anne got the tea and had made wonderful hot biscuits. "I must say, Anne has turned into a real smart girl," Mrs. Lynde told Marilla when Anne left the room. "She must be a great help to you."

"She is," said Marilla. "I would trust her in anything now."

"I didn't think she'd turn out so well that first day I was here," Mrs. Lynde said. "Mercy, I shall never forget that tantrum! But it's wonderful how Anne has improved over the years—especially in her looks. I'm happy to admit that I made a mistake about Anne."

~ 22 ~
The Next Year

Anne enjoyed her summer. She and Diana almost lived out-of-doors, and Anne walked, picked berries, and dreamed to her heart's content. When September came, she was bright eyed and ready to study.

Miss Stacy's Queen's class began to worry they would not pass the exam. Anne dreamed that Gilbert Blythe's name was at the top of the pass list, but that her name was nowhere on it.

But it was a happy, busy winter. Anne was active socially, too. Marilla now let Anne go on outings occasionally. There were concerts and parties and sleigh drives and ice-skating.

Anne loved all of the activities, and she grew quickly during the year. One day Marilla was surprised to find that Anne had grown taller than her. Marilla felt a little sad. The child she had learned to love was gone and here stood a tall, serious-eyed girl of fifteen. Matthew found Marilla thinking by the fire that evening.

"Anne has gotten to be such a big girl," she said to Matthew. "She'll probably be away from us next winter. I'll miss her terrible."

"She'll come home often," he said, trying to comfort Marilla.

"But it won't be the same." She sighed gloomily.

There were other changes in Anne. She became much quieter, too. "I just don't like to talk as much," she explained to Marilla. "It's nicer to keep thoughts in one's heart like treasures."

"It's only two more months until the entrance exam," said Marilla. "Do you think you're ready?"

Anne shivered. "I don't know. Sometimes I think I'll be all right, and then I get horribly afraid. What if I don't pass?"

"You could go back to school and try again," Marilla answered.

"I don't think I'd have the heart for it," said Anne. "It would be such a disgrace to fail, especially if Gil—if the others passed."

Anne sighed and dragged her eyes away from the spring outside and looked at her books. There would be other springs, but if Anne did not pass this exam, she was not sure she could enjoy them.

~ 23 ~
The Pass List Is Out

With June came the end of school and the end of Miss Stacy's role as a teacher there. The children were very sorry to see her go.

Anne and Diana walked home after their last day. It won't be the same next year with Miss Stacy gone and you and Jane and Ruby probably," Diana said. "We've had jolly times, haven't we, Anne?" Two big tears rolled down by Diana's nose.

Diana's crying set off Anne's tears.

"If you could stop crying, I probably could stop, too," Anne replied. "If I don't pass this exam, I'll be back next year with you."

"But you did well on the exam Miss Stacy gave," said Diana.

"Yes, but that exam didn't make me nervous," Anne said with a smile.

Anne went to town and started the examination Tuesday. English was first and then history. Anne thought she did well on English, but knew she'd mixed up a few dates in history. On Wednesday, Anne had geometry.

By Friday, Anne was back at Green Gables and was

happy it was over. Diana was waiting for her. "It seems like ages since you left," cried Diana. "How did the exams go?"

"Pretty well, I think," she said, "in everything but geometry. I don't know whether I passed or not. We'll know soon when the pass list is out."

"Oh, you'll pass all right," said Diana.

"If I don't come out high up on the list," said Anne, "I'd rather not pass at all." And Anne felt she would not be successful unless she beat Gilbert Blythe.

During the examination days in town, Gilbert and Anne had passed each other on the streets and pretended not to see each other. Anne had held her head high, but she wished a little more that she had made friends with Gilbert when he had asked her. She knew that all of Avonlea School was wondering who would come out first. Anne felt she would be humiliated if she were not first on the list.

But Anne had a better reason to do well. She wanted to make Matthew and Marilla proud. Matthew had said she would "beat the whole island." Although Anne thought that was too foolish to hope for, she did want to be among the top ten students. Anne so wanted to see Matthew's kind eyes gleam with pride in her work.

Anne began to walk to the post office every day in hopes of seeing the pass list in the newspaper. But day after day, there was nothing. After three weeks, Anne felt that she could not stand waiting much longer. Then the news came.

Diana came flying up the slope, fluttering a newspaper. Anne sprang to her feet, but she couldn't move. Diana burst through the door.

"Anne, you've passed!" she cried. "You've gotten first place—you and Gilbert both. It's a tie!"

Sure enough, there was Anne Shirley's name on the top of the list of two hundred. That moment was worth living for. Anne could not say a word.

"Everyone from Avonlea passed," Diana continued. "Won't Miss Stacy be proud? I am pretty near crazy with excitement, but you're calm and cool, Anne."

"I'm dazzled inside," Anne finally said. "I never dreamed I could beat the whole island. I must tell Matthew."

So they ran out and found Matthew, Marilla, and Mrs. Lynde outside. "I've passed and I'm first—or one of the first!" Anne said.

"Well now, I always said it," said Matthew gazing at Anne with delight. "I knew you could beat them easy."

"You've done pretty well," Marilla said, trying to hide her huge pride from Mrs. Lynde's critical eye.

But Mrs. Lynde said kindly, "We're all proud of you, Anne."

~ 24 ~
The Hotel Concert

A nne was dressing for the concert at the White Sands Hotel. The guests were having a concert for charity, and they had searched for performers. Anne was one of them.

Matthew was very proud that Anne was selected to recite. Marilla was almost as proud, though she did not tell Anne.

"Do you think the organdy dress is best?" asked Anne.

"It looks as if it grew on you. It's perfect," Diana said. "There's something so stylish about you, Anne. Perhaps it's the way you hold your head. There, you're ready."

Marilla appeared in the doorway. She was much thinner now and had grayer hair, but her face was softer. "Anne, you look neat and proper," she said. Marilla went downstairs, thinking she was sorry she couldn't see Anne recite tonight.

"I'm going to miss my little room when I go to school next month," said Anne longingly as she looked around her room. "I can see the sunrise every morning over the hills from this window."

"Please don't speak of your going away tonight,"

begged Diana. "I don't want to think of it, it makes me so miserable. Are you nervous about tonight, Anne?"

"Not a bit. I've recited so often in public now," Anne said.

But when they arrived at the hotel, Anne felt suddenly shy and self-conscious about being from the country. Her dress that had seemed so pretty back at home now felt simple and plain. Other women were dressed in fancy silks and lace with big jewels. Anne shrunk into a corner.

On the platform in the concert hall, Anne felt even worse. She was standing next to a tall lady in pink silk, who looked down on her. Another woman in white lace kept talking to her neighbor about "country bumpkins" and how much fun it will be to see the local people perform. Anne could not wait until it was all over.

To make matters worse, a professional had agreed to recite that night. She was staying at the hotel. She had dark eyes and was dressed in a gown of shimmering gray. The audience went wild over her performance. Anne listened in awe. When the woman finished, Anne thought she could not perform after her. *Why did I ever think I could recite?* thought Anne miserably.

Then Anne's name was called, and she moved dizzily out to the platform. Diana and Jane clasped their hands together nervously. Anne realized she had never before had an audience like this, and the sight of all the people made her freeze. Her knees trembled, her heart fluttered, and she could not utter a word.

But suddenly, her eyes saw Gilbert Blythe in the audience. Anne drew a long breath and flung her head up proudly with determination. She *would not* fail in front of Gilbert Blythe! She began to recite in a strong, clear voice. Anne recited as she had never done before. And when she finished, there was a burst of applause.

Anne went back to her seat. The lady in pink clasped her hands. "You did splendidly! They're encoring you to come back!"

Blushing, Anne went back to give a funny little selection that entranced her audience even further. When the concert was over, the lady in pink introduced her around to the people she knew. Everyone was very kind to Anne.

"There was an American sitting behind me," Diana said on their way home. "He asked who the red-haired girl was. 'She has a face I would like to paint,' he said. Isn't that a nice compliment?"

"Yes, I suppose it is," Anne said with a laugh.

"Your recitation was simply great," Jane said. "You were better than the professional. And did you see all of the diamonds on her? Wouldn't you just love to be rich, girls?"

"We *are* rich," Anne said firmly. "We are happy as

queens, we have sixteen years to our credit, and look at the sea—all silver tonight. We wouldn't enjoy it more if we had ropes of diamonds. I'm happy to be Anne of Green Gables."

~ 25 ~
A Girl at Queen's

During the next three weeks, Anne got ready to go to Queen's. Matthew made sure that Anne had pretty dresses to wear. And for once, Marilla did not object to anything that needed to be bought.

Marilla had a fancy green dress made up for Anne to wear to parties. It had just as many tucks and frills as everyone else's dresses, too. Anne put it on one evening for Matthew and Marilla. As Marilla watched, she thought about the frightened child who arrived at Green Gables only a few years before. Tears came to her eyes.

"Are you crying, Marilla?" asked Anne in disbelief. She gave Marilla a kiss on the cheek.

"I was thinking of the little girl you used to be, Anne," Marilla answered. "You've grown up now and you're going away. You look tall and stylish—so different in that dress. I got sad thinking about you leaving Avonlea."

"Marilla!" Anne sat down on her lap and took Marilla's lined face between her hands. "I'm not changed, really. It won't make any difference where I go or how different I look. In my heart, I will always be your little Anne. And I will always love you and Matthew and Green Gables."

Marilla wished then she could express her feelings like Anne, but she couldn't. Marilla could only put her arms around Anne and hold her close, wishing she didn't have to let go.

Matthew talked with Marilla downstairs when Anne was in bed. "Anne is smart and pretty and loving, too, which is better than all the rest. She's been a blessing to us. There never was a better mistake than the one Mrs. Spencer made. And I don't believe it was luck. I think the Almighty saw we needed her, plain and simple."

The day came when Anne left for town. After a tearful good-bye with Diana and Marilla, Matthew drove her to town. Marilla worked fiercely around the house in the afternoon with a bitter heartache. That night she knew there was no little girl at the end of the hall. Marilla couldn't help sobbing miserably into her pillow.

Anne arrived in town and soon met her professors and all the new students. She decided to take up second-year work, as Miss Stacy had advised. Gilbert Blythe did the same. This meant they could get their teacher's licenses in one year instead of two. But it also meant harder work and more of it.

As it turned out, Gilbert Blythe and Anne were in the same class. This was comforting to Anne since they could keep up their old rivalry. *Gilbert looks very determined*, Anne thought when she saw him. *I suppose he's made up his mind to win the medal.*

Anne was lonely, though, in the beginning. That first night she went back to her boardinghouse room and felt homesick as she looked around her dull little room. She missed the view out her window at Green Gables.

Just then Josie Pye knocked on her door. "I'm so glad you came," Anne said sincerely.

"I'm not going to be homesick," Josie said. "Town is so exciting after little Avonlea. Do you have anything to eat? That's why I came."

Anne was wondering if being tearful and lonely was better than being with Josie Pye. Then Jane and Ruby arrived. Ruby asked right away if Anne was thinking of trying for the medal. Anne blushed and said she thought that she would.

"And Queen's is going to get one of the Avery scholarships after all!" said Josie excitedly. "It will be announced tomorrow."

An Avery scholarship! Anne's heart beat more quickly. She pictured herself winning the scholarship and going to Redmond College. She knew that the winner would need the highest grades in English literature. With hard work, she might be able to do it. *Won't Matthew be proud of me if I win it?* she thought.

~ 26 ~

Working Toward
the Dream

Anne's homesickness went away after a while. It helped to have several weekend visits to Avonlea. Gilbert Blythe almost always walked Ruby Gillis home from the train on Fridays. "I wouldn't think she was the sort of girl for Gilbert," whispered Jane to Anne.

Anne could not help thinking that it would be nice to have Gilbert as a friend. They could talk about books and studies and what they wanted to do with their lives. Gilbert was a clever boy. Ruby told Jane that she didn't understand half the things Gilbert Blythe said. He talked just like Anne Shirley, she'd said.

Anne made friends and worked hard at the academy. It was thought that the medal winner would be one of three people—Gilbert Blythe, Anne Shirley, or Lewis Wilson. The Avery scholarship was more doubtful, with six people who might win it.

Soon spring arrived and exams were taken. There was so much work and activities to do that the end of the school year fairly flew by. On the morning they were to find out the examination results, Anne and Jane walked down the street together.

"I don't have the courage to go look at the results," said Anne. "Jane, would you read the announcements and then come tell me?" Jane agreed, but as they started up the steps of Queen's, they saw Gilbert Blythe being carried on the shoulders of a crowd of boys. "Hooray for Blythe, Medalist!" they cheered.

For a moment, Anne felt sick with disappointment. She had failed, and Gilbert had won! Well, Matthew would be sorry. But then someone called out—

"Three cheers for Miss Shirley, Avery winner!"

"Oh, Anne," gasped Jane. "Isn't it wonderful?"

And then the girls were around them and Anne was the center of a laughing, congratulating crowd. She was hugged again and again, and her hand was shaken dozens of times.

"Oh, won't Matthew and Marilla be pleased!" Anne said.

Graduation soon arrived, and Matthew and Marilla were there to see Anne. As the Avery winner, Anne read her essay and was pointed out and whispered about in the audience.

"Reckon you're glad we kept her, Marilla?" asked Matthew when Anne finished reading.

"It's not the first time I've been glad," Marilla said.

Anne went home to Avonlea with Matthew and Marilla that evening. She simply could not wait another day. Diana was at Green Gables to meet her. "Oh, Diana, it's so good to be back again," Anne said. "And it's so *good* to see you! I love you more than ever, and I've got so many things to tell you."

"You've done splendidly, Anne," said Diana. "I suppose you won't be teaching now that you've won the Avery?"

"No, I'm going to Redmond in September," Anne said.

"Gilbert Blythe is going to teach," Diana said. "He has to. His father can't afford to send him to college next year, after all, so he will have to work his way through. I think he'll get the school here."

Anne felt strange. She hadn't known this. She had thought Gilbert would be going to Redmond also. What would she do without their rivalry?

The next morning at breakfast it suddenly struck Anne that Matthew did not look well. He was much too gray. "Marilla," asked Anne quietly, "is Matthew well?"

"No, he's not," said Marilla in a troubled tone. "He's had some real bad spells with his heart this spring, and he won't cut back on his work. I'm real worried about him. We've got a good hired man now, so I'm hoping he'll rest and pick up a bit. Maybe he will now that you're home. You always cheer him up."

Anne leaned across the table and took Marilla's face in her hands. "You are not looking well either, Marilla. You look tired. You must rest now that I'm home. I'm just going to take this one day off to visit old friends, and then it will be your turn to be lazy."

Marilla smiled gently at Anne. "It's not the work so much as my head," she said. "I've got pain so often now behind my eyes. There is a well-known oculist coming to the island, and the doctor says I must see him. But enough about that—have you heard anything about the Abbey Bank lately, Anne?"

"I heard that it was shaky," answered Anne. "Why?"

"That's what Rachel said. There was talk about it. Matthew felt real worried since all we have is in that bank—every penny."

Anne put her hand on Marilla's shoulder. She said she'd go out now and be back to help Marilla later. Outside it was bright and everything was in bloom. Anne never forgot that day. She visited all her most loved places and many friends. In the evening, she went with Matthew for the cows. Matthew walked slowly with his head bent while Anne stood tall and erect.

"You've been working too hard today, Matthew," Anne said carefully. "Why don't you take things easier?"

"Well now, I can't seem to," he replied.

"If I had been a boy," said Anne, "I'd be able to help you now."

"I'd rather have you than a dozen boys, Anne," said Matthew, patting her hand. "Well now, it wasn't a boy who took the Avery scholarship, was it? It was a girl — my girl I'm proud of." He smiled his shy smile at her and went into the yard. Anne took that memory with her and kept it close to her heart for a long time.

~ 27 ~
Death Comes to
Green Gables

"**M**atthew—what is the matter? Are you sick?"
Marilla spoke with alarm in every word.
Anne came through the hall with flowers
in her hands. She was just in time to see Matthew
standing on the porch with a folded paper. His face was
strangely drawn and gray. Anne dropped her flowers
and sprang across the kitchen to him the same moment
that Marilla did. But they were both too late. Matthew
had fallen over across the porch.

"He's fainted," gasped Marilla. "Anne, run for
Martin—quick! He's at the barn."

Martin, the hired man, went for the doctor, going
first to the Barrys' house to send them over to help.
Mrs. Lynde, who was at the Barrys', came too. They
found Marilla and Anne bent over Matthew.

Mrs. Lynde pushed them gently aside and felt for
Matthew's pulse. Then she laid her ear over his heart.
She looked at them sadly as tears came to her eyes.

"Oh, Marilla," she said sadly. "I don't think—we
can do anything for him."

"Mrs. Lynde, you don't think—you can't think Matthew is—is—" Anne couldn't say it. She felt sick.

"Child, yes, I'm afraid so," Mrs. Lynde said.

When the doctor came he said Matthew had died at once and probably did not feel any pain. It could have been from a sudden shock, he said. When they read the papers that Matthew had in his hand, they discovered what had caused the shock. The letter told of the failure of Abbey Bank. All that Marilla and Matthew had was gone.

The news of Matthew's death spread quickly through Avonlea. Friends and neighbors poured into Green Gables and brought food for Marilla and Anne.

The Barrys and Mrs. Lynde stayed with them that evening. Diana went to Anne and said gently, "Would you like me to sleep here with you tonight, Anne?"

"No, thank you, Diana," she said. "I think I want to be alone. I haven't been alone since it happened—and I want to be. I want to be quiet and try to realize it. Half the time it seems to me that Matthew can't be dead."

Marilla had sobbed in great storms all day. But Anne had been silent. Anne hoped that tears would come when she was alone. It seemed to her a terrible thing that she could not cry for Matthew. She had loved him so much, and he had been so kind to her. All day she had had a dull ache of misery.

In the night, Anne awakened with the stillness

about her. The sorrow of the day came over her in a wave. She could hear Matthew saying, "A girl—my girl I'm proud of." Then the tears came and Anne wept bitterly.

Marilla heard Anne and crept in to comfort her. "There, there, don't cry so, Anne," she said.

"Oh, what will we do without him, Marilla?" Anne sobbed.

"We've got each other, Anne," Marilla said. "I don't know what I'd do if you weren't here. Oh, Anne, I know I've been strict with you, but you mustn't think I don't love you as well as Matthew did. I want to tell you now when I can. It's never been easy for me to say things about my heart. But I love you as much as if you were my own flesh and blood. You've been my joy and comfort ever since you came to Green Gables."

Two days later they carried Matthew Cuthbert over the fields and the orchards that he loved, and he was buried. Then Avonlea settled back into its own routine. Even at Green Gables, life went on. There was work to be done, but it was done with an aching sense of loss.

"It feels I'm being disloyal to Matthew to find pleasure in things now," Anne said to Mrs. Allan one evening. "I miss him so much—and yet, the world is still interesting and beautiful to me. Today Diana said something funny and I found myself laughing. I thought that I would never laugh again."

"When Matthew was here he liked to hear you laugh," said Mrs. Allan. "Even though he's gone, he still likes to know you can find happiness."

They talked a while and then Anne got up to leave. "I must go home now. Marilla gets lonely at dusk."

"She will be lonelier still, I'm afraid, when you go away to college," said Mrs. Allan.

Anne did not reply. She said good night and went slowly home to Green Gables. When she entered the yard, Anne found Marilla on the porch steps.

"Doctor Spencer was here," Marilla said. "He says I must see the specialist in town tomorrow about my eyes. Will you be all right while I'm away?"

"Yes," said Anne.

Then Marilla and Anne talked about all the students from Avonlea and what they were doing next year.

"Jane and Ruby are going to teach, and they both have schools," Anne reported.

"Gilbert Blythe is going to teach, too, isn't he?" Marilla asked.

"Yes," said Anne shortly.

"What a nice-looking boy he is," said Marilla. "I saw him in church last Sunday. He looks a lot like his father did at that age. John Blythe was a nice boy.

People used to call him my beau."

Anne looked up with interest. "Oh, Marilla—what happened?"

"We had a quarrel. I wouldn't forgive him when he asked me to. I meant to, but I was angry. He never came back. But I always felt rather sorry. I kind of wished I'd forgiven him when I had the chance."

"So you had a bit of romance in your life," said Anne softly.

"Yes, I suppose I did," replied Marilla.

~ 28 ~
A New Beginning

Marilla went to town the next day. Anne went to visit Diana and returned to find Marilla sitting at the table with her head in her hands. Something about the way she sat sent a chill to Anne's heart.

"Marilla, did you see the oculist?" Anne asked anxiously.

"Yes, he said that if I give up all reading and sewing entirely and any kind of work that strains my eyes, and if I'm careful not to cry, he thinks my eyes won't get worse and my headaches will go away," Marilla said. "But if I don't, he says I'll be blind in six months. Blind! Anne, just think of it!"

For a minute, Anne could not speak. Then she said bravely, "Marilla, *don't* think of it. The doctor has given you hope. If you are careful, you won't lose your sight altogether."

"I don't call it much hope," said Marilla bitterly. "What am I to live for? I might as well be blind— or dead. As for crying, I can't help it when I get lonesome."

When Marilla had eaten, Anne got her to bed. Then

she went to the east gable and stared out her window into the darkness. Anne's heart was heavy. How much things had changed since she had sat there the night she came home! Anne had been full of hope and joy then. She felt she had lived years since that night.

But when Anne went to bed, she had a smile on her face. She had realized her duty and found a friend in it.

A few days later, Marilla came in from the yard where she had been talking to a man Anne did not know.

"What did that man want?" Anne asked.

Marilla sat down. There were tears in her eyes and her voice broke. "He wants to buy Green Gables."

"Buy Green Gables?" Anne wondered if she had heard correctly. "Marilla, you don't mean to sell it!"

"Anne, I don't know what else to do. If my eyes were strong, I could stay here with a good hired man. But I can't now. Oh, I thought I'd never see the day when I'd have to sell my home! Every cent of our money went into that bank. I'm thankful you're provided for with that scholarship, Anne. I'm sorry you won't have a home to come to on your vacations, but I suppose we'll manage."

Then Marilla broke down and cried bitterly.

"You mustn't sell Green Gables," Anne said.

"I wish I didn't have to," she replied. "But I'd go crazy with loneliness and my sight would go if I stayed here."

"You won't stay here alone," Anne said firmly. "I'll be with you. I'm not going to Redmond."

"Why, what do you mean?"

"Just that," said Anne. "I'm not going to take the scholarship. I decided the night you came home from town. I can't leave you alone after all you've done for me, Marilla. I've been making plans. I'm going to teach. I've applied for the school here, but I don't expect to get it since the trustees have promised it to Gilbert Blythe. But maybe I can have the Carmody school. And I'll read to you and keep you cheered up. We'll be cozy and happy here together, you and I."

Marilla had listened to Anne like a woman in a dream. "Oh, Anne, I could get along real well if you were here. But I can't let you give away the scholarship for me."

"Nonsense!" laughed Anne merrily. "There is no sacrifice. Nothing could be worse than giving up Green Gables. My mind is made up, Marilla. I'm *not* going to Redmond."

"But your ambitions—"

"Oh, I'm just as ambitious as ever," said Anne. "Only my ambitions have changed. I'm going to be a good teacher, and I'm going to save your eyesight. I plan to study here at home and take a college course all by myself. Oh, I've got lots of plans, Marilla."

"You blessed girl!" Marilla exclaimed. "I feel

you've given me a new life."

When it became known of Anne's new plans, there was much discussion around town about it. Mrs. Lynde paid a visit to Green Gables not long after.

"Did you hear I'm going to teach at Carmody?" Anne asked.

"Well, I don't know," she replied. "I think you're going to teach right here in Avonlea. The trustees are giving you the school."

"Mrs. Lynde!" Anne squealed and sprung to her feet. "Why, I thought they'd given it to Gilbert Blythe!"

"So they did. But when he heard you had applied for it, he told the trustees he wouldn't take the job and suggested you instead. He's going to teach at White Sands. Of course, he did it because he knew you wanted to stay with Marilla. He made a big sacrifice since he'll have to pay for a room in White Sands—and he has to pay his way through college, you know."

"I don't think I ought to take it," Anne said softly.

"Well, Gilbert has signed the papers with White Sands, and it won't do him any good if you refuse to take Avonlea now."

Anne went to put fresh flowers on Matthew's grave the next evening. She stayed for a while until the sun started to go down. Walking home, Anne saw a tall boy come whistling by the Blythe property. It was Gilbert, and he stopped whistling when he saw her.

Anne stopped and held out her hand.

"Gilbert," she said with red cheeks, "I want to thank you for giving up the school for me. It was very good of you—and I appreciate it."

Gilbert took her hand eagerly. "I was pleased to help. Are we going to be friends now? Have you really forgiven me?"

Anne laughed. "I forgave you that day by the pond, although I didn't know it. How stubborn I was! I've been sorry ever since."

"We were born to be friends, Anne," said Gilbert with a smile. "I know we can help each other in many ways. Are you going to keep up your studies? So am I. Come, I'll walk you home."

Marilla looked curiously at Anne when she entered the kitchen. "I didn't think you and Gilbert were such good friends that you'd stand for half an hour at the gate talking," she said.

"We haven't been—we've been good enemies," Anne said. "Were we really there half an hour? It seemed just a few minutes. But we have five years of lost conversation to catch up on, Marilla."

Anne sat gazing out her window that night. The wind purred softly through the arms of the cherry tree and she could see Diana's light through the orchard. Anne was happy and content.

"All's right with the world," she whispered.